Is It Too Windy Back There, Then?

A COMPENDIUM OF
PHRASES WE HEARD GROWING UP

By Janet Letnes Martin & Suzann (Johnson) Nelson

Printed in the United States of America.
Published by Caragana Press
Box 396,
Hastings, Minnesota 55033

Library of Congress Catalog Card Number 96-084249
ISBN 1-886627-01-0
First Edition

DEDICATION

**THIS BOOK IS DEDICATED TO
THE FIRST BATCH OF
RURAL BABY BOOMERS,
AND ESPECIALLY TO THOSE LIKE US,**

—JANET, SUZANN AND THE TRUCK ON THE COVER—

WHO TURNED 50 THIS YEAR!

TABLE of CONTENTS

Dear Moms, Dads, Children and Others of the Midwest,

Here we are at the Levee Cafe in Hastings, MN again, site of inspiration for the Introductions of our past successes: *Cream Peas on Toast, They Glorified Mary - We Glorified Rice,* and *They had Stores - We had Chores*.

On the way here from Janet's house (she drove), Suzann sat in the backseat — where old women with sensible shoes belong — and we tested the wind velocity. From this field research we can report that IT IS TOO WINDY BACK THERE, THEN at 32 miles per hour if even only one front window is open. Of course, the air was a little nippy as Fall is coming to the Midwest so any breeze creeping in was uncomfortable compared to, well say like a Saturday night in July

July coming home from the drawing in town and Jimmy's ice cream is running down the side of the cone and dripping on the floormat right where Darrel dropped his cotton candy that he bought from the lady with dangly red earrings who wore too-short short-shorts whose maiden name was Haugen but you've forgotten her first name and you feel a hotflash coming on and at the same time remember that Carolyn has forgotten to memorize the Meaning of the Second Article for tomorrow.

Of course, testing wind velocity in town isn't an exact science. There are a number of variables to consider like:

- the streets are paved so no dust blows in your eyes making it seem worse than it really is,

- one doesn't wear a heavy kerchief in town,

- there are no big farm trucks zipping by creating wind like in the country,

- there are no tractors pulling a 6-bottom to slow you down and give you some relief from the breeze,

- do or don't you have a Cocker in the front seat with his head out the window acting as a partial buffer?

- to what extent do stores lining the streets compare to shelter belts?

- how many wing windows are cracked open a bit, and if both front windows are open, then consider where exactly you are sitting in the backseat, the speed of the car, whether or not the driver guns the engine or slips the clutch, what direction the wind is really coming from and, if you have a station wagon, is the back window open a little bit to let out bees?

If you are truly Midwestern and like to save words like you save used Christmas paper, you now know – because of our thorough research – how close you can put the pedal to the metal without asking the standard question: IS IT TOO WINDY BACK THERE, THEN?   If your speedometer is broken or it is too dusty to read, you know it is too windy back there, then, if:

- the hair stands straight up on the Cocker Spaniel,

- Donna's popbeads fly open,

- Widow Snustad, who is getting a ride with you to Family Night, puts her pleated rain bonnet on over her beaded hairnet,

- the Mr.'s carpenter pencil flies off his ear,

- someone in the backseat asks "What's that you say, then?" and you haven't said anything,

- the cubbyhole door flies open and the ball of twine (usually located next to the *snus* can) falls out,

- Elroy spits *snus* out his window and it comes back in landing on the Mrs.'s clean anklets and wedgies and when she bends over to wipe it off

with a hanky (the one with a hand-crocheted border
she got for Christmas from her secret partner in
Sewing Circle), Baby Jimmy tips off her lap hitting
his head on the N-S-E-W ball on the dash and his
chin on the throttle,

- the netting on Grandma-from-Goodhue Township's
corsage starts to unravel and the red carnations
begin to wilt,

- the chaff and dust on the armrests start whirlwinding
around and the church bulletin from the last Sunday
in April flies off the back window ledge,

- the kid sitting next to you loses his wind,

- you miss the full text of a Burma Shave sign or can't quite read how many more miles it is to Wall Drug.

If these situations remind you of how things used to be — back in the era of sensible shoes and decent meals — this Compendium is for you! Save your voice, strain your eyes, test your memory, and laugh your head off! (Norwegian-Lutherans don't need many body parts anyway).

There are several **WARNINGS TO THE READER** that we feel compelled to mention:

- **Put a breeze bonnet on if you are going to go over something similar to the Old Spiral Bridge in Hastings, MN,**

- **Bring at least a see-through kerchief and a vial of homemade eyedrops if you will be leaving the car to check the fields,**

- **The only excuse for excessive speeding is when city cousins come to visit the farm and your big brother drives all you kids on the tummy-tickler road, and**

- **This book is best read aloud, preferably by one with a genuine, rural Scandinavian-American brogue!**

Three 50-Year-Olds,

Janet and Suzann and the Truck on the Cover*

* (Thanks to **Donald L. Dee Trucking**, Lansing, IA)

We have drifts as high as the brooder house!

Back before Doppler radar, before climatologists with hair-pieces and too much make-up, and before 24-hour weather channels, old folks with arthritis predicted the weather two days in advance, wind direction was tested with spit on a finger, and any man worth his salt could read a barometer.

If your parents ever reminded you that they walked six miles one way to school in the middle of a blizzard (and you refrained from telling them that it was dangerous and stupid), if you know what "town homes" are, and if you ever spent a few hours on a summer evening in a storm cellar, then the following memories, photos and phrases will keep you occupied during the next Alberta Clipper.

Cover your face.

It's too windy to burn the ditches.

It's gonna be a real humdinger.

She's a corker.

There's too much dew to combine.

Oh, it's good sleeping weather.

Guess we're ready now. He's banked the house.

Mrs. Lloyd Studlien, Napkin Collector, Nov. 5, '58,
Lake Mills, IA

Does it feel a little drafty in here?

I'm just going to take the chill out a little.

Ja, she's beastly kaldt ut!

Plug the heater in.

Pull your chair up to the oven and put your feet in.

She's coming outta the West.

Doesn't that air feel good?

You can see your breath.

"Is it hot enough for you?"
said at 97° above by Virgil Olson

"Is it cold enough for you?"
said at 40° below by Virgil Olson

"Is it hot in here or is it just me?"
said off & on by Virgil's Mrs.

I'm roasting.

Hold on to your hat!

Fill in your favorite phrases:

Stay off that pond. The ice isn't thick enough.

Jack Frost has been at the window.

There'll be frost on the pumpkin tonight!

Culvert must be plugged again.

It's gonna run over the bank.

The bridge washed out.

Watch your feet. It's slippery.

Don't eat yellow snow.

If your tongue sticks to it, don't blame me.

Don't put your tongue on the flagpole.

Don't put your tongue on the pump handle.

Uffda, the air is so heavy. She sure came up fast.

Hail pounded the wheat down on its side. It's all lodged.

It stripped the corn clean off the cobs.

We had hail the size of golf balls over here.

It sounded just like a freight train was comin' through.

The walleyes should be biting after this blows over.

It's too wet to plow,
*   too windy to haul rocks,*
*   might as well dance...*

(unless you're Lutheran)!

Plain or peanut butter?

Back before consolidation, open enrollment, vouchers, interactive TV and classes in cultural diversity, kids sat in alphabetical order and grew up reading about Puff jumping and Dick running, diagraming sentences, and passing Palmer Penmanship exams.

If you can remember lining up with your parents for the Brand New Oral Polio vaccines, sitting under your desk during civil defense drills, and if you can recite at least four verses from Longfellow's <u>Song of Hiawatha</u> these photos and phrases will put you at the head of the class where you've always belonged.

Do you have to go Number One?

Put up two fingers if you have to go Number Two.

Now put on your Thinking Caps.

Let's play house. No, Let's play doctor.

Let's go play fort.

Let's play sticks.

No, let's play dishes.

Now learn it by heart and play it by ear.

Kilroy was here.

She's practicing driving in the pasture.

It's my turn!

"No, you don't need tennis shoes. You can just go stocking-footed in the gym. Who do you think you are, Marilyn Monroe?"

Vernon Kvernen to his daughter, Janice, Sept. 4, '58

Get up right now. You can stay in bed as long as you want when you get old.

She's pretty owly this morning.

Don't eat the paste.

Stop, Look, Listen!

They're out of chocolate milk.

He's got snot running outta his nose.

Let me use your corkgrease.

Fraidy Cat!

How would you like it if I did that?

If you can't say anything good, don't say anything at all.

Speak up. Don't mumble.

Do it right the first time.

Don't ever write something down you don't want someone else to read.

Did he make you parallel park?

Hum your pitch.

Weenie!

Keep your hands to yourself.

Finish practicing piano before Gabriel Heatter comes on.

Have you finished your homework and practiced your flute?

Ja, they're sure rambunctious at this age.

He had to stay after.

Put the tail below the line.

Are you a whistler or a whiner?

I can't see the blackboard.

Pull down the shades. We have a filmstrip.

What were you doing in the cloakroom?

Fill in your favorite phrases:

A place for everything and everything in its place.
Miss Fititude, 4th Grade Teacher, Arnegard, ND, Feb. 8, '57

One more time and you'll have to sit in the corner with the dunce hat on.

Who has the pitch pipe?

Practice your flashcards with a partner.

Mavis, are you in Group 1 or Group 2?

Are you in the Red or the Blue Reading Group?

He's yanking my braids!

He's snapping my bra.

I'm gonna tell.

Oh grow up!

"Do you have your Weekly Reader and lunch money?"

Everyone's Mom Every Monday

Have you found a Current Event?

Don't forget to bring your dental card.

Will you get this through your thick skull?

How many times do I have to tell you that?

Go outside and clean the erasers.

Send me a note.

Show me your hands.

No throwing spitballs.

I broke my reed.

Quit picking your nose.

That's my name. Don't wear it out.

Don't be so dumb!

We just went over that.

They must be going steady.

They're kinda on again, off again.

"He just 'sends' me!"
Phyllis Fjoslien, Frederic, WI, Sadie Hawkins Day, Nov. '59

Did he kiss you?

Back before drip-dry, combination windows and no-wax floors, "Men worked from sunrise to setting sun, but women's work was never done."

If you know the original meaning of "She's hanging out" and "They're separating," and if you're still canning 48 pints of beet pickles just in case, and you're still washing and waxing the floor on your hands and knees so you can get in the corners good, then these photos and phrases should jar your memories right out of the cellar.

Get me the bowl and a clippers.

Catch that rain water so we can have soft water to wash our hair.

It's a good day to clean.

Check the burners.

Put it down.   Pick it up.

Empty the slop pail.

Take out the chamber pot.

What do you do for potato bugs?

Don't walk on the floor until I put newspapers down.

I'm sending you some clippings from the paper.

Watch where you put your feet.

Wipe your feet off.

Squish that boxelder bug.

Take the ashes out.

"Get it in cold water, QUICK!"

**Bernice Skragness to her son Melvin at the closing Sunday
School picnic held at the City Park in Park River, ND**

Don't get mud on the rug.

*Scrape your four-bucklers off
before you come in.*

Thread this needle for me.

Wash up now! I just put clean sheets on.

Don't let it boil over.

Aren't you gonna cart that outta here?

You hang that laundry up properly now or what will the neighbors think?

Put it back where you found it.

Pick up your clothes.

Do you smell gas?

I'm just going to beat the band.

Did I unplug the iron?

Shake the rugs.

Grab me a clean apron. Some-one's coming.

Here comes the Watkins man.

Here comes the Stanley man.

Hide that. The pastor's coming.

"It's tough on a woman when things go haywire."

Agnes Hanson, Eastern North Dakota Synod, '54

Fill in your favorite phrases:

All I do is work...

We gotta clean house 'cuz you never know when someone might come!

Did you hang the storms?

Air out the house.

Do it now. You can't work on Sunday.

Bring in wood.

Go pick the eggs.

They had it so cozy.

They fixed it up so nice.

"Uffda Lars,   the sheets smell so good, don't they? Oh Lars, don't the sheets smell fresh?"

Lily Hovde, Underdahl, MN April 6, 1951

Where's the fly swatter?

Oh ja, she's just cookin' up a storm.

Don't push on the screen.

Get some fresh water.

I heard she got a Mix Master.

Barrows and gilts up two, slaughter lambs down one,
pork bellies unchanged, heifers and steers steady!

Back before people paid good money to go to petting zoos, before school kids took field trips to farms, before cats ate "gourmet" foods, and before yuppies and lonely women bought exotic birds that had been captured by heathens, we had our own personal zoos. They were called barns.

Cows, horses, sheep, pigs, kittens, barn swallows and flies all lived in harmony under one roof until we needed to eat one. Here are some photos and memories for those of you who have sheared a sheep, castrated a pig, butchered a steer, or curry-combed a horse, and who know the true meaning of the saying, "Quit running around like a chicken with its head cut off"!

How big is the herd?

How many you milking, then?

She's 'bout ready to calf.

How much is she givin'?

Time to re-shingle the chicken coop.

Did you water the chickens?

Come Boss, Come Boss.

Here Kitty, Kitty, Kitty, Kitty...

Have you done the chores?

You done with the milking?
Cows can't wait.

Did you put down the bedding?

Gutters shoveled out?

"Take it to the creamery."

Alice Severson, who always thought she needed extra spending money for frivolous things, to her daughter, Sharon, May '53 Stoughten, WI

She's all dried up. He put her out to pasture.

Get some DDT and spray the barn.

Don't go near the bull and watch out for the electric fence.

"If you're not going to work with her more than that, you're never going to get a blue."

Dorothy Gustafson, rural Hatton to Ronny, before 4-H Achievement Days in Mayville, ND, August, '53

Where's the curry-comb?

Did you slop the pigs and throw down some hay?

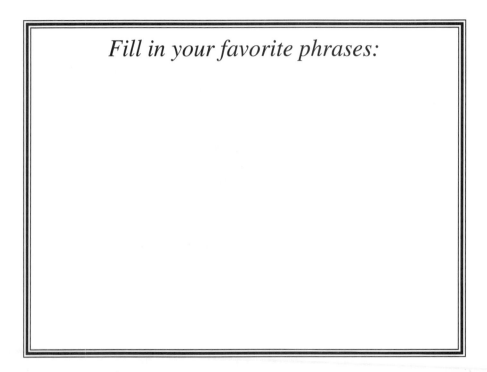

Fill in your favorite phrases:

Bring it to the locker plant.

Did you wash out the separator?   Did you change the filter disk?

Is the bulk truck coming?

Scrape your boots off.

Call the rendering truck.

The cows are out!
The cows are out!

He's cultivating over by Emil's!

Back before combines were air-conditioned, before pickups had cell phones and the before the noon market report came across on the computer:

> *"Work was work, and*
> *Work was real, and*
> *Men took a nap,*
> *After The Meal.*

The year was divided into four different seasons: Planting, Haying, Harvesting, and Winter for Fixing. Similarly, the food groups were divided into Dairy and Meat in the barn, Grains in the granary, Fruits and Vegetables in the garden or cellar, freshly Baked Stuff in the pantry, and Snacks in town.

Town people who lived in town and didn't own property wasted time and money on lodge memberships, bowling, and movies magazines. They had it pretty good but back on the farm, from "Sunrise on the swamp" until way, way past bankers' hours, we knew that *"The early bird catches the worm,"* *"We ain't got all day, you know,"* and *"It's a tough row to hoe."*

Here are some photos and memories for those of you who came from a family that made its living off the land.

Hitch up the stoneboat.

I gotta help Dad pick rocks.

Pull hard and it will come easy.

He brought the two-banger over to Henry's.

Scour the bottoms.

Plow until dark.

Did you cover the exhaust pipe?

He's got a self-propelled.

"A couple cheese sandwiches and some 'yinyer' snaps will be fine."

Dad

"Fill the 'Termos' and a water jug for Dad, and take lunch out to the men and don't play near the machinery."

Mom

I'm gonna take a short snooze before I go back out. You listen for the noon market report.

Put her in the stanchion when I leave.

Park the spring-tooth by the shelter belt on the West 40.

I'll give you a nickel for every 100 mustards you pick.

"He's stuck in the North Slough up to the lug bolts!"

La Ferne Heskin in reference to her husband La Verne, to the County Agent who just dropped in, somewhere in Central Wisconsin in '55.

We're just gonna drive around and look at the fields.

His rows look like he's spelling Sivert Sivertson.

Have you greased her up yet?

Hitch her up.

Time to move on to Tostenson's.

Fill in your favorite phrases:

The wind just ripped that binder canvas right in two.

"Uff, this barley can get itchy."

Ingvald Sjursrud to the rest of the threshing crew, rural Sidney, MT, 1939-1951

Don't lose the hitch pin.

The windrows are too wet.

The oats are lodged.

Ja, the buckwheat looks good, but she smells awful.

We finished up the North 40.

How many bushels per acre you gettin'?

He kept the men on after harvest.

Bring the Allis over to Leo's.

It's got padded seats.

Bring me the tin snips.

*Gotta get the snow fence up
before she flies.*

It doesn't smell spoiled!

Back before microwaves, "deep freezers," and food processors, women baked with lard, "put up" with pressure cookers, candled eggs, and made cake from scratch. Women made breakfast, lunch, dinner, lunch, supper, lunch, and it was "Come in, Sit down, 'Vær så god'" for drop-in company. Meals were served at the table, in the field, and in the church basement.

If someone at your table ever mumbled "It's too tomatoey," here are some photos and phrases to jog your memories of flypaper, chokecherry jelly, elbow macaroni (that was cooked in whole cow's milk) served with either sliced wieners floating around in it or with a side of fried Spam, and lunches that were topped off with either rhubarb or gooseberry sauce.

Just a small piece. Oh, they're all small.

It smells like something's burning.

They're so easy to can.

Don't choke on the bones.

Oh, I just brought some pantry pickles.

"Cut them smaller. They'll go farther. There's more at this funeral than we expected, considering his character and everything."

Selma Swenson of the Ruth Circle, '50

Just add a little more water.

Just take a little in case there isn't enough.

I think you've had enough.

Just cut the bruises out.

Check the burners.

On, she's just cookin' up a storm.

It'll keep.

It shouldn't spoil that fast.

Say when!

My, that's great plenty.

Did you make enough food?

I think we'll just have leftovers.

Just help yourself, then.

What's for dessert?
Rhubarb sauce again?

Fill in your favorite phrases:

I put up 32 quarts.

It's easy for her. She's got a deep freeze.

Check the pressure cooker gauge.

We'll have to use it up before it spoils.

Keep your fork.

Do you want more coffee?

Do you take it black?

"What in the world should I do with all these organdy aprons?"

Pearl Braaten to her 7 grownup daughters (who had lots of high school friends and had been waitresses at many weddings right after graduation) in May 1956 when they all made it home for Mother's Day

Well, if that don't take the cake!

Don't talk with food in your mouth.

Think of all the starving kids in China.

Just be glad we got something to eat.

Wipe it off and eat it anyway. A few germs aren't going to kill you.

Clean up your plate.

Can we have seconds?

The Hovland Twins, Cresco, IA

Don't lean back in your chair.

Look how skinny she is. She's gotta put some meat on those bones.

Will you have a cold drink?

"I scream, you scream, we all scream for ice cream."
Gjertrud Kringen's 5th Grade Sunday School Class

Just add a pinch of this and a handful of that.

I guess I make it just "by gosh and by golly."

Pack a lunch.

Clear the table.

Did you check the stove?

Shuck those peas and snap those beans before noon.

"How many pitchers of nectar do we need?"

Mrs. Esther Anderson, July Refreshment Committee Chairman,
First Lutheran Church, Estherville, IA, July 4, 1952

Don't slam the door. I've got an angel food in the oven.

Get a couple of lugs. We'll put some up for winter.

Don't choke!

Have you polished the shoes for Sunday yet?

Back before the Gap, Limited and Target, there were no high couture trunk shows or megamalls. Mannequins made fashion statements in the windows of the S & L, Herberger's and J.C. Penney's, and we had 4-H and Home Ec Style Reviews. Normal looking models wearing homemade circle skirts, jumpers and aprons came down the runway (a series of tables from the school lunch room which had been lined up to come off the stage and right down the center line in the gym where the basketball co-captains, Howard and Jerry, shook hands with the ref and the guys from the other town just down the road apiece) that had been covered with white butcher paper which wrinkled and ripped and then tripped the models.

Alane, the high school chorus's accompanist (see the book <u>Cream Peas on Toast</u>...) who had gone beyond John Thompson Book Three, played her recital pieces and a medley of 'Under the Apple Tree', 'Cindy Oh Cindy', and the 'Moonlight Sonata' throughout the Review. This was the only peaceful thing happening.

Behind the blue or maroon velvet stage curtains there was a flurry of activity as friends checked:

- if seams were straight,
- if darts were even,
- if anyone was slippin',
- if basting threads and stick pins had been

removed, and
• if underarm shields were holding up.

Here are some phrases to trigger your memories of the two classes of clothes — Everday and Church — that were often homemade or hand-me-downs, but had been sprinkled and starched to make one look spiffy and stunning anyway!

What kinda get-up you got on?

Your part's crooked.

At least you could look clean!

She just had a perm.

It's "snowing down South."

There they were, wiggling down the street in tight skirts dressed like street walkers and looking like painted ladies, and skipping Junior Chorus practice.

Oh, good. You wore flats too.

Now wear a kerchief and take your handkerchief.

Just hold your pants on.

Turn it inside out and wear it over.

Do you have a hanky?

Save it for the clothing drive.

I don't care if it's old-fashioned.

Wash that paint off your face.

Did you press the seams flat?

Get your bangs outta your eyes.

Get that hair outta your eyes.

Don't wear that. I just washed it.

You're too young for nylons.

"Don't get that. You'll stand out. Get something where you'll blend in more."

Mrs. Gilbert Mortenson to her daughter, Delores, at the S & L in Waterloo when they were selecting a dress for Confirmation and Public Questioning.

There's nothing to sewing that.

I just ran my good nylons.

Your plaids don't match up in the seams.

Pack a rain bonnet.

Better get your storm coat.

Buckle your boots up.

Your shoes are all scuffed.

Don't walk on your shoes.

Your strap's showing.

You don't need anymore can-cans.

Your buttons are one off.

If you're gonna wear those see-through dresses, put your slip on. I can see right through you.

I wouldn't be caught dead in that!

Did it shrink?

Is it washable?

Have you grown that much?

Where's your FFA jacket?

You could see his crack!

You can't wear plaids and stripes.

You can't wear white shoes before Decoration Day.

Put your white shoes away now. Labor Day is over.

Stay outta my purse.

No, you can't wear his Letter Jacket.

I'll wear my good girdle under it.

He lost his cuff link at League.

Change your clothes.

Where did that hole come from?

Did you get ink on that shirt too?

Where are my scuffs?

It just doesn't go.

Roll up your cuffs some more.

Save that for church.

Put your earlaps down.

I hate long brown stockings.

I hate garter belts.

Now practice wearing heels.

Put a book on your head.

Don't split your seams.

Your hem is coming down.

Fill in your favorite phrases:

Put your corduroy pants on under your skirt.

It's cold. Get your bloomers out.

They fit good enough and that's that!

You got a new Christmas dress last year.

I'll make you one. I can sew one cheaper.

I don't care if it's out of style; it will keep you warm.

You're not old enough for a bra.

That's way too short.

"Someone took my rubbers at Brotherhood."

Alvin Eng, Member of Nidaros Lutheran, Vining, MN

She took "blue" on her apron.

Those are way too high.

Uff, she looks a fright!

I'm just lost without it.

Who do you think you are, Jayne Mansfield? Wear something baggier!

His suspenders are twisted.

I bet she's got falsies.

Are you going to enter 'Make It With Wool'?

Just stuff some Kleenex® in there. Who'll know?

You'll grow into it!

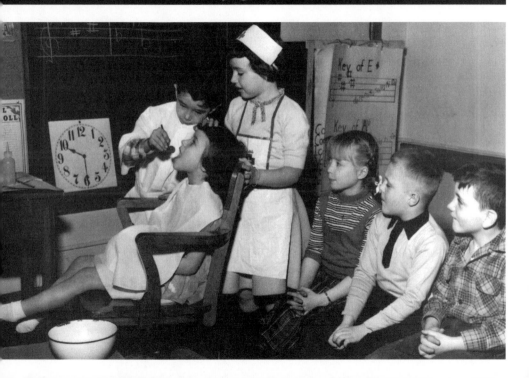

Back before paracervical blocks, home pregnancy kits and sick-to-their-stomach new dads in birthing rooms, women either had a bun in the oven or one under the apron and had Harvey call Bertha when they "took ill."

Ringworm was rampant, mercurochrome and iodine took care of almost everything, and Watkin's Carbo-Salve — covered with a hunk of cloth held in place with white adhesive tape that you cut with your teeth — took care of the rest.

The County Nurse struck as much fear and reverence in a kid as the Lutheran Minister or a

Catholic Nun.

If you've been feeling a little under the weather lately but certainly not sick enough to go to the doctor's office, and if you are old enough to have a small pox vaccination mark, the following photos and phrases are just what the doctor ordered.

They put the boys in one room for a film with the coach and the school nurse met with us and gave us these little plastic bags.

She looks like she swallowed a watermelon seed. Is she PG?

He's got a tickle in his throat.

She's got a frog in her throat.

You'll live. It'll heal.

It might be the croup. S'pose it could be worse, though.

If he keeps holding his Sunday socks up with garters, he'll get varicose veins.

"Sugar diabetes runs in his family."

Lydia Ness talking about Clarence Kville. (Lydia had a second cousin who was a nurse in Aberdeen, SD)

She's feeling so poorly that she's doctoring in town now.

They're handing out goiter pills at school in Wisconsin again.

Uffda, I tell you, she could just eat like nobody's business.

She's starting to show.

He's on the wagon.

How's your flow?

She can't. Her cousin's coming to visit.

Do you have to go toidy?

Do you have to tinkle?

Don't sit on the toilet seat.

Do you need more peach papers down there now?

Wash your hands after you tinkle.

Fill in your favorite phrases:

Write me an excuse for gym class.

No wonder she's PG. They're always necking.

A poultice should take care of that festering.

This won't hurt a bit.

Did the county nurse check you for headlice?

He's lookin' too peaked to be perky.

There's enough dirt in your ears to grow corn.
Traill County Nurse, Nov. 8, '54

I'm just all tuckered out.
Traill County Nurse, Nov. 9, '54

Don't put anything in your ear smaller than your left elbow.

Don't use your shirtsleeve.

Is that a boil on the back of your neck?

Brush it 100 strokes.

Brush your shoulders off.

Scrub your elbows with Lava.

Don't run with a scissors or a sucker in your mouth.

Don't touch anything at the county fair. You never know who has touched it before you.

Put your head between your knees.

Wash your neck or you'll get ringworm.

Steele County Nurse, Nov. '54

Did you get behind your ears?

I s'pose you could get by with just a sponge bath or a spit bath.

Plug your ears and gulp water.

Did you have a bm?

**Midwestern male physicians to
Norwegian-American Lutheran female patients.**

Get out the cloves.

She's all black and blue.

Soak it in Lysol.

Cover your mouth.

Alfred looks like he's three sheets to the wind.

No one ever died from hard work.   (Ja, sure!)

Just use some soda.

"Don't come in soakin' wet. You know consumption and gout run in the family."

Klara Kjos to her son, Willard, every day it looked like rain around Mabel, MN

You're going to have to wash more than just your hands and face!

Sven's Mrs. is a little under the weather.

It seems like Ida feels kind of blue.

Don't squeeze that pimple. It might turn into a scar.

Get that sliver out before it starts to fester.

Button up or you'll catch your death from a cold.

I think we'll call it a day.

Let the clutch out when I wave!

Back before there were dual airbags and anti-lock brakes, "Made in Japan" meant junk, not good cars. Families of 10 had two cars; a good one for church* and an uninsured one for the field. The Sunday cars were washed for Easter, and the clunked-out field cars were put out to pasture in the grove to rot and to rust. (Most of them are still there).

Catholics were identified by St. Christopher statues on the dashboards of station wagons, Protestants by the N-E-S-W ball on the dashes of sedans, and Hoods by dangling dice in their hotrods as they dragged Main and displayed Chesterfields in their rolled up tee-shirt sleeves.

Here are some phrases and memories for those of you who have ever cranked it, "put on" gas, used a throttle or a steering knob (with a rose or flag superimposed in it), or know what it feels like to stand on the running board while she kicked up dust on the gravel road.

*The good car was used for going to town on Saturday night for the drawing, for church and going visiting on Sunday, and by the confirmed boys so they could go to the Junior-Senior Banquet. (The J-S Banquet is the same thing as a Prom in The City, but without dancing).

I'm just looking to see.

Ya betcha. She's a humdinger!

No foolin'. She's a dandy!

It smells like burning rubber in here.

"Grind me a pound while you're at it."
Maynard Holkesvig to his nephew, Norvald the Confirmand, as he taught Norvald to drive.

You'll be able to just feel where reverse is.

Just use the ten and two position.

Put her in neutral.

Just keep it between the ditches.

Watch where you're going.

Drive careful!

Don't pop the clutch.
    Don't slip the clutch.
Don't ride the clutch.
    Don't ride the brake.

Put the handbrake on.

Park her in back.

Go practice your driving in the cow pasture.

"Mom, can I drive from the mailbox?"

**Linda Larson, High School Cheerleader,
Blooming Prairie, MN '58**

She's overheated.

You don't have to burn the carbon out every time you take the car.

Harvey's Dad

What's it got? Three on the tree or four on the floor?

He bent the jack.

Is it too windy back there, then?

Fill in your favorite phrases:

Just go North ahead for about two miles and turn at the Olson farm, just kitty-corner from Tollefson's barley field, and there she'll be.

Directions given to the new Dakota County Agent, the new one who didn't know his way around yet.

They got a two-tone four-door.

She wouldn't turn over. We had to crank it.

Choke it a little, but don't flood it.

Put some cardboard in front of the radiator.

Looks like we'll need chains.
Any North Dakota County Agent in Any January.

A fella could get lost in those ruts!

The running boards are rusting out.

"Jeepers, Creepers. Here come the boys from South Dakota."

Someone from a border town.

He's got a steering knob with a pretty lady in it.

Don't cross the county line.

Idle threats by rival hood gangs.

There he was, comin' smack dab in the middle of the road!

He's looking at one that is all souped up.

He was going 60 per.

He drove like a bat outta hell.

Check out those spinners.

Spitshine the whitewalls.

Let's neck.

Back before state-sponsored lotteries, hot tubs and syphoning off good pasture land for golf courses, people knew that "a penny saved was a penny earned," "a fool and his money are soon parted," and"the love of money is the root of all evil." Diapers weren't disposable but became good rags, and good rags became rugs. We didn't need a county bulletin to tell us where and how to recycle. We just did it from the slop pail to the "string too short to save."

If you ever ironed your used Christmas wrap for the next year, packed sandwiches in a cereal box liner or knew how to stretch Jell-O, then these photos and phrases won't be going to waste.

Well, it's good enough for me.

We're not like the rest.

You start it, you finish it.

We didn't have much money but we had love!

"I suppose you get that way when you get old."

Gladys Bjørkelien, about her husband Melvin's aunt in 1953 at the bridal shower for Melvin's only neice, Donna, who had been up for Princess Kay from their region .

Save the eggshells for the African violets.

Here. I darned your sock.

You'd think she lived in Hollywood.

**Alma Ostlund about her floozy neighbor, Violet Smith,
who had relatives "Back East."**

Bring the Sears and Roebuck to the outhouse.

I just gave you a new Band-Aid yesterday.

Don't waste Kleenex°! Just use a hanky. If God wanted you to have Kleenex° he wouldn't have given you a hanky.

Nils Olson who had a tough time "reading for the Minister," Parkers Prairie, MN

Melt down those soap scraps.

Oh, just wrap it in newspaper.

We'll send the overshoes to the foreign mission fields. They'll just have to be thankful for what they get.

Paper Plates? Do you think you're the Queen of England?

Can I have a slip of that ivy?

You called her long-distance in the middle of the day?

We can grease the cookie sheets with that.

Well for Heaven's Sake! Don't throw it away!

Don't waste good water. Don't waste good food. Don't waste time. Waste not, want not.

It's perfectly good still. She works good as new.

Not today. It's not on sale.

Do you have a coupon for it?

They're the kind of people that throw out stuff that's perfectly good still.

Is that all there is?

Don't use so much!

Just use a little so it will last longer.

<u>Boughten</u> cat food???   What next!

Oh, he just dickers and haggles over a few pennies.

You'll just have to grow into them.
Now say thank you.

Fill in your favorite phrases:

"Before you cut rags, cut off the zipper and buttons."

Alvhild Bottolfson at the Elm Lake Lutheran Church in Maddock, ND when they were making quilts for the Foreign Mission Field

Why, you haven't even worn out your other one yet.

Send me a penny postcard.

Don't just throw the tinsel on.

Don't tear the wrapping. We can iron it and use it over next year.

Don't spend it all in one place.

Buy the cheapest you can find.

Prices are sure going up. I wonder where they'll end?

You paid how much for that???

They're gonna price themselves right outta business.

How much water are you putting in the tub anyway?

Don't flush it every time.

I'll put it away in case I have to go to the hospital.

Call at night when the rates go down.

You don't have to call home unless something really bad happens.

It's getting too dark to read.

You're not going to run to town and waste gas for just one little thing.

That should do her.

Just Act Decent!

Before adults began to encourage feuding kids to "take time out," before parents gave kids an allowance for cleaning their rooms (which was just plain expected and showed common sense), and before trend-setters and "human service providers" wanted everyone to "share their feelings" and then thanked them for it, kids were to be seen and not heard and expected to sit up straight, behave, act decent and Turn Out! Parents were parents and not their kids' buddies. Parents acted their ages and expected kids to act older than theirs. They married for "better or for worse" and stuck to their vows. Ringworm was more prevalent than divorce, and counseling wasn't part of the pastor's job even though stoking the church's coal furnace was.

Now pay attention!

"I could just wring his neck."
Melba (Chicken Lady) Torkelson from rural Story City, IA
after she found out her son had decided not to go to Luther.

Stay out there and watch the burning barrel.

You understand me?

Says who?

Well? Spit it out!

Oh, make sense now.

I have half a notion to paddle you.

I told you not to get hurt.

Catch my drift?

Get that cat outta here.

I've told you 100 times, that is a BARN cat.

Santa Claus is watching you!

You understand me?

"Watch out for the electric fence and don't go near the bull."

Mrs. Henry Heskin, 4-H Group Leader near Starbuck, MN

If that's the way it is, then that's the way it is.

Shut the door. Were you born in the barn?

Where've you been? You smell like smoke.

Said by Gloria Estenson's mother when Gloria came home late from the basketball game with what looked like a hickey.

Listen here, smarty pants. I've just about had it!

What makes you think you're so good then?

Don't get on my nerves.

Just Snap Outta It!

Put a scarf over your face.

Don't forget your mittens.

Put your boots on.

Don't lose your mittens.

Stay away from the tracks.

Wash your hands.
Don't put your elbows on the table.

How will you get big like me if you don't eat all your food?

Clean up your plate.
Clear the table.

Behave.
Behave in public.
Behave in town.
Behave in church.
Behave yourself.
Behave yourself, then.
Just behave now!

Fill in your favorite phrases:

You'll have H-E-double toothpicks to pay!

Don't put your nose on the window.

Blow your nose.

Mind your manners.

Stand straight.
Don't slouch.
Sit up.
Sit still.
Keep still.
Don't be late.
Put it away.
Pick it up.

Put that down.
Shame on you.
Cut it out.
I said, No!
We'll see.
Never mind.
Oh, be decent, now.
That's it!

"I'll give you something to cry about."

Hjelmar Kringen, every day in 1955 and 1956 when his daughter, Barbara Sue, an only child, would whine and sniffle about one thing or another.

When we get there, be quiet and behave cuz she gets so nervous, you know.

Someday you'll thank me.

Say thank you.

Did you say thank you?

Get on up to bed.

Don't walk on the floor.

Oh, whatever.

Enough said.

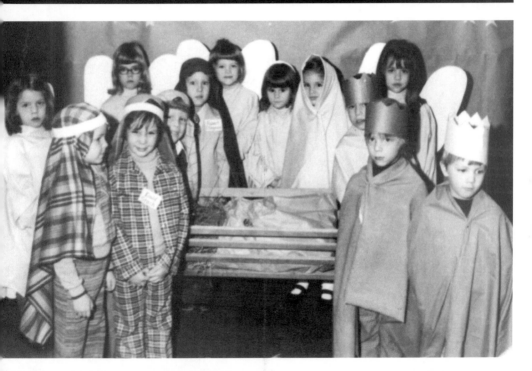

Just the singing parts; no angels or shepherds.

Back before the Crystal Cathedral and before the green hymnal and support groups and liturgical dances in church, there were chalk-talks, flannelgraph stories, Fireside Hour, Dorcas, shuffleboard for the youth, Brotherhood for the men, and Ladies Aid in the afternoon with a good lunch. Confirmation classes were two hours every Saturday morning for two years and included sessions on the Evils of Dancing and Turning.

If you know the significance of What Does This Mean? and How Is This Done? or the source of "To Belie, Betray and Backbite," then these photos, memories and phrases are "Most Certainly True."

NOTE TO THE READER:

TO MAKE YOU FEEL MORE COMFORTABLE

WITH YOUR REVIEW OF RURAL LIFE IN THE

'50S, THE AUTHORS FELT IT WAS APPROPRIATE

TO HAVE THE CHURCH SECTION PRINTED IN

"BLACK HYMNAL" SCRIPT

Well, no wonder his barn blew down. He was doing field work on Sunday.

"Guess we blew a fuse again."

***Every December at the Lutheran Church's
Lutefisk Supper in Jamestown, ND***

Is it Communion Sunday again?

Learn it forwards and backwards by heart before tomorrow morning.

Why is she always fanning herself with the bulletin, even in January?

𝕳e's home on furlough."

Emma Satterlie talking about Gen Larson's son, Ivan, who looked so good in his uniform. (Gen looked as proud as could be, too). Veteran's Day Sunday, '54.

𝕸y, you'd think they could've given a little more.

𝕾he's got quite a brood.

Should we give the church a little extra?

I don't care how you feel. You've got perfect attendance & you're gonna keep it up!

Is nothing sacred anymore?

Do you have your Sunday School offering?

Let me tie it in your hanky so you don't lose it.

Do you have your Birthday pennies?

Shut your eyes. Fold your hands.

They live in town and don't own property.

You can thank your lucky stars you aren't one of them.

You don't need a new suit if you're only in church at Christmas and Easter.

Get one now. It can always be your funeral suit.

Let me straighten your tie.

She got a new 'do' for Easter.

You can't wear that to church; we have altar offering.

Take your Easter dress off before you spill red nectar on it.

*Get home early.
There's church tomorrow.*

Fill in your favorite phrases:

If it's good enough for the pastor, it's good enough for you.

Why does it always smell so musty down here?

Should I wear a hat?

Just the cup. Not the saucer.

*Said to Hjalmer Peterson as he tried to grab
both the cup and saucer from Myrtle Nelson
who was pouring at Ole and Anna Swenson's
Golden Wedding Anniversary, June 28, '49*

Let's hurry up and get going so we can hurry up and get home.

There were skads of people there.

Tent Revival Meeting
July 31, '48
Benson, MNt

Are you going to dress up for the Luther League hayride?

I know I'm not wearing high heels.

When are we going to clean the parsonage?

It's my turn to serve.

Whose turn is it to take the towels home?

Is this your pan?

Put your initials on it next time.

I always keep a pair of funeral shoes handy for serving at church doings.

They put her in The Home.

Well, when your time's up, your time's up.

Mrs. Axel Olson explaining to
her grandson why the
hired man died.

ACKNOWLEDGMENTS

Photo Credits

Cover Photo

    Bill Tate – Canton, MN – Photographer

    Donald L. Dee Trucking – Lansing, IA – Truck

Chapter 1 Divider

    Larry Aasen – Westport, CT – Personal Collection

Chapter 9 Center Photo

    Hawley Herald Collection (Dairy Princess Candidates)

    Clay County Historical Society, MN

Minnesota Historical Society

Pedestrians Fighting Wind, St. Paul Dispatch-Pioneer Press
Hot Lunch Program at Inver Grove
Cloakroom and Elementary Classroom – Richfield
    Photography, Inc.
Women Leaning Against a Haypile – Bloomington
Inver Grove School Home Canning
Sewing Area / Home Economics Classroom – Richfield
    Marshall Weinberg Photography, Inc.
Dentist Office – Longfellow School, St. Paul

ORDER FORM for <u>Is It Too Windy</u>

Name_____

Address_____

City_____St_____Zip_____

(Canada $9.95)

No. of Copies_____ @ $7.95   **Subtotal:$_____**

Plus **Postage & handling**   per book

    1st Class $2.00 per book $_____

    Book Rate $1.50 per book $_____

(Maximum postage cost for multiple orders: $6.00)

MN residents add 6.5% **sales tax** $_____

Send cash, check or money order to:

    Caragana Press   **TOTAL: $_____**
    Box 396
    Hastings, MN 55033

ORDER FORM for <u>They Glorified Mary</u>

Name_____

Address_____

City_____St_____Zip_____

(Canada $8.95)

No. of Copies_____ @ $6.95　　　　**Subtotal:$_____**

Plus **Postage & handling**　per book

　　1st Class　　$2.00 per book　　　　　　　$_____

　　Book Rate　　$1.50 per book　　　　　　　$_____

(Maximum postage cost for multiple orders: $6.00)

MN residents add 6.5% **sales tax**　　　　　　$_____

Send cash, check or money order to:

　　Caragana Press　　　　　　**TOTAL: $_____**
　　Box 396
　　Hastings, MN 55033

ORDER FORM for <u>They Had Stores</u>

Name_____

Address_____

City_____St_____Zip_____

            (Canada $9.95)

No. of Copies_____ @ $7.95   **Subtotal:$_____**

Plus **Postage & handling**   per book

    1st Class $2.00 per book $_____

    Book Rate $1.50 per book $_____

(Maximum postage cost for multiple orders: $6.00)

MN residents add 6.5% **sales tax** $_____

Send cash, check or money order to:

    Caragana Press   **TOTAL: $_____**
    Box 396
    Hastings, MN 55033

ORDER FORM for <u>Cream Peas on Toast</u>

Name_____

Address_____

City_____St_____Zip_____

(Canada $11.95)

No. of Copies_____ @ $9.95   Subtotal:$_____

Plus **Postage & handling**   per book

   1st Class $2.00 per book $_____

   Book Rate $1.50 per book $_____

(Maximum postage cost for multiple orders: $6.00)

MN residents add 6.5% **sales tax** $_____

Send cash, check or money order to:

   Caragana Press   **TOTAL: $_____**
   Box 396
   Hastings, MN 55033

FOR COPIES OF **OTHER BOOKS and PRODUCT**S by
Janet Letnes Martin, or to be on
the mailing list, write to:
Martin House Productions
Box 274
Hastings, MN 55033

FOR INFORMATION ABOUT **PROGRAMS and**
SPEAKING ENGAGEMENTS by ONE or BOTH
of the CARAGANA PRESS CO-AUTHORS, CALL

Janet Letnes Martin   OR   Suzann Nelson
@ 800-950-6898   @ 800-494-9124

or WRITE:
CARAGANA PRESS
Box 396
Hastings, MN 55033

ORDER FORM for <u>Uffda, But Those Clip-Ons Hurt</u>

Name_____

Address_____

City_____St_____Zip_____

(Canada $6.95)

No. of Copies_____ @ $4.95   **Subtotal:$_____**

Plus **Postage & handling**   per book

    1st Class $2.00 per book $_____

    Book Rate $1.50 per book $_____

(Maximum postage cost for multiple orders: $6.00)

MN residents add 6.5% **sales tax** $_____

Send cash, check or money order to:

    Caragana Press   **TOTAL: $_____**
    Box 396
    Hastings, MN 55033